CAMBODIA

VIRUNGA
NATIONAL PARK
CONGO

Havana CUBA

The next time
I come home,
I promise we'll
find an adventure Te Quiero
together!
El Capitán

AUSTRALIA

GUINEA

BIG BEND
NATIONAL PARK

THE FARALLON ISLANDS

Mis queridos,
I'm coming home.
I think this
was my last
real adventure. Nos vemos pronto,
El Capitán

NTARCTICA

日本 Sotomo Arch

For my parents and LB—the greatest adventures
are shared with the ones you love.

Library of Congress Control Number: 2017054167

ISBN 978-1-338-13419-3

10 9 8 7 6 5 4 3 2 1   18 19 20 21 22

Printed in China 38
First edition, September 2018

The type was hand lettered by the artist.

The art for this book was made using a Wacom Cintiq
and Adobe Photoshop plus handmade textures.

Book design by Charles Kreloff

the GREATEST AdVENTURE

by Tony Piedra

☗ Arthur A Levine **Books**

an Imprint of

Scholastic Inc.

Eliot was a great adventurer.

After it rained,
he sailed the high seas.

And in the shadows,
he tracked the trails of wild beasts.

But just as things were getting good...

and his adventures would end.

Eliot wanted something real.

Then one day, Eliot's grandfather, El Capitán, sailed home.

He told Eliot stories about real
adventures on his boat, the Hispaniola...

Passing through jungle rivers

and sailing over deep, dark seas.

Eliot was enchanted.

And the next morning, he was ready for a real adventure, too.

So El Capitán led Eliot into the wilds of the city to find one.

PARKING

They discovered concrete giants.

They stalked a paper dragon.

They were swept up by a plastic sea.

But Eliot saw no jungles.
He saw no sharks or whales.
He saw no real adventures anywhere.

"We can take out your boat!"
Eliot blurted.

El Capitán let out a deep breath.
"We can't, mijito—
but I'll show you why."

But Eliot was sure with a little work,
she could be perfect again.

"Grandpa, haul in the anchor!
Fasten the hatches!
All aboarrrd!"

"Are you ready to find an adventure?"

And what they found
could not have felt more real.

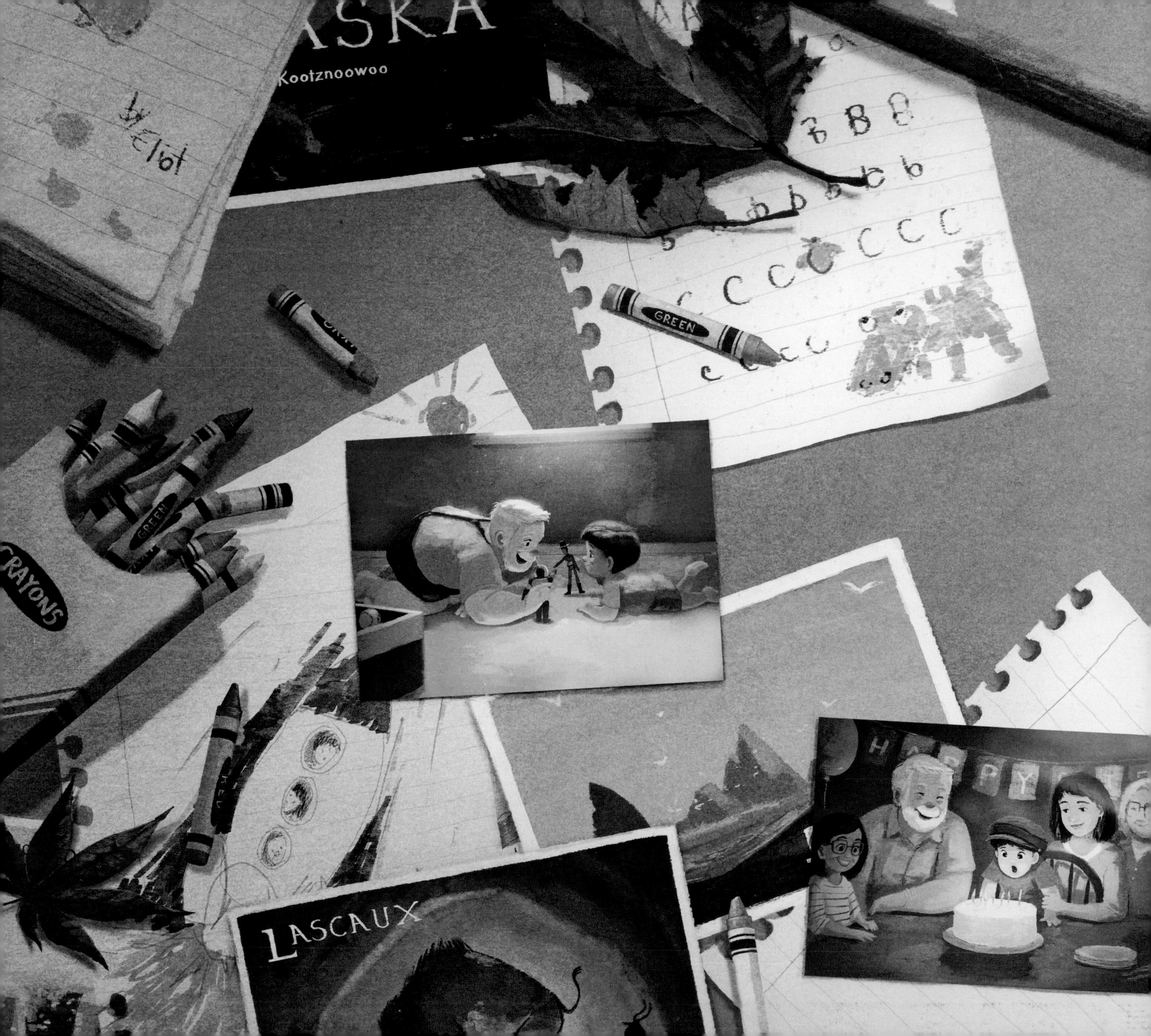
ASKA
Kootznoowoo
GREEN
GREEN
CRAYONS
RED
LASCAUX
HAPPY